My Best Friend

My Best Friend

WRITTEN BY Gilles Tibo
ILLUSTRATED BY Janice Nadeau

SIMPLY READ BOOKS

Published in 2018 by Simply Read Books
WWW.SIMPLYREADBOOKS.COM
Text © 2007 Gilles Tibo
Illustrations © 2007 Janice Nadeau

LIBRARY AND ARCHIVES CANADA CATALOGUING IN PUBLICATION

Tibo, Gilles, 1951-
[Ma meilleure amie. English]
    My best friend / written by Gilles Tibo ; illustrated by
Janice Nadeau.

Translation of: Ma meilleure amie.
ISBN 978-1-77229-022-6 (hardcover)

    I. Nadeau, Janice, illustrator II. Title. III.Title: Ma meilleure
amie. English

PS8589.I26M313 2018   jC843'.54   C2018-901182-3

We gratefully acknowledge for their financial support of our publishing program the
Canada Council for the Arts, the BC Arts Council, and the Government of Canada.

Originally published in French in 2007 by Les Éditions Québec Amérique Inc, as
Ma meilleure amie.

Manufactured in Malaysia.
French edition art direction by Isabelle Lépine.
English edition book design by Heather lohnes.

10 9 8 7 6 5 4 3 2 1

To my best friend…

Death

I don't want to brag, but I know Death very well. She's not a man. And she's not a woman. She's a shadow that roams the corridors of a hospital. She passes through the walls. She goes in and out of the rooms and sometimes she leaves holding a child in her arms.

In the beginning of my hospitalization, when I was very sick, I called Death often to come look for me. I listened for her. When she was approaching, I whispered to her, "Hey, Death... I'm here... Take me with you, if you would like..."

But Death never even turned; she always continued on her way. Until one evening when she appeared at the foot of my bed. She didn't even breathe. Her eyes were fixed on me. Her back bent.

At that moment, I was feeling less sick. I don't want to brag, but I said this to Death: "Come back another evening. If you are tired, you can rest here, in my room."

To my surprise, Death sat at the end of
my bed. We didn't exchange a word. I
was a little scared. I didn't know what to
say or do. I offered her a glass of water.
She refused by shaking her head, "no."
I sipped a few times, then fell asleep.
When I woke up, Death was gone.

The Visits

The second time Death came to visit me, she accepted a few sips of water.

The third time, she drained the glass because she was very thirsty. She had just taken a child, an adult and an old man to the land of dreams. Her hands were shaking. I think she was sobbing a bit. To loosen the tension, I asked her, "The land of dreams, where is it?"

Death didn't respond. She lifted her head and looked straight into my eyes. That's when I understood something important. Death was sad.

During the long days, I thought a lot about Death. I wouldn't want to change places with her. Why? Because, first, everyone hates her. Death, she is never invited for a bike ride. She's not even welcome at the lake or in an amusement park. If by some misfortune Death finds herself in one of these places, it's because there was an accident. A drowning or a broken ride.

Second, Death must work twenty-four hours, seven days a week. No days off, no holidays. And Death is never congratulated for her work.

And third, Death is all alone in this world. No father. No mother. No friends. She never watches TV because she has no home. Death shivers in winter and dies from heat in summer.

"Being Death, that's not a life," I whispered to her in the dark.

She didn't respond. But she smiled.

The Bed

Last month I changed rooms three times but Death always found me easily. In fact, now she comes to visit more often. Why? Because I'm the only one who doesn't hide when she appears. I'm the only one who talks to her, offers her water.

Death doesn't sit at the end of my bed anymore. Now she sits in the middle of it, next to me. We share an apple or an orange, or a piece of cake. While eating, I tell her about my life. "Today, the doctors changed my perfusion. My parents came to visit me. I received a present, a little truck."

Every time I talk to Death, she lifts her shoulders a bit. She laughs sometimes.

It's not easy being friends with Death since she doesn't talk much. I ask her questions and she answers only "yes" or "no." When my questions bother her, she pouts. When this happens, so Death will forgive me, I make jokes. I say, "Me, I want to live like I'm dying— of laughter…"

The Surprise

I don't want to brag, but Death now sits next to my head and comes to see me very often. I talk to her into the early hours of the morning. I talk to her about everything and nothing, but mostly about my toys because this makes her feel good.

I try to find some tricks to surprise her. One evening, to fool Death, I play dead in my bed. Death approaches. I don't move. I don't breathe. Death looks at me, scared, touches my forehead, which I have wiped with cold water. Death doesn't understand anything anymore. Thinks I'm dead for real. Just when she starts to tremble, I wake up yelling, "SURPRISE!"

Death jumps so high she bangs her head on the ceiling and cries, "Eeeeeeh!" so loudly that the nurses come running into my room.

Quickly, Death hides under my bed.

I tell the nurses that I had a terrible nightmare. They come around me, kiss me on my face and leave, closing the door of my room. Very angry, Death comes out from under my bed rumbling, asking me never to do that again.

I say I'm sorry. Death forgives me, taking me in her arms. We both cry.

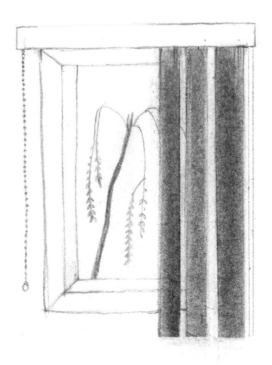

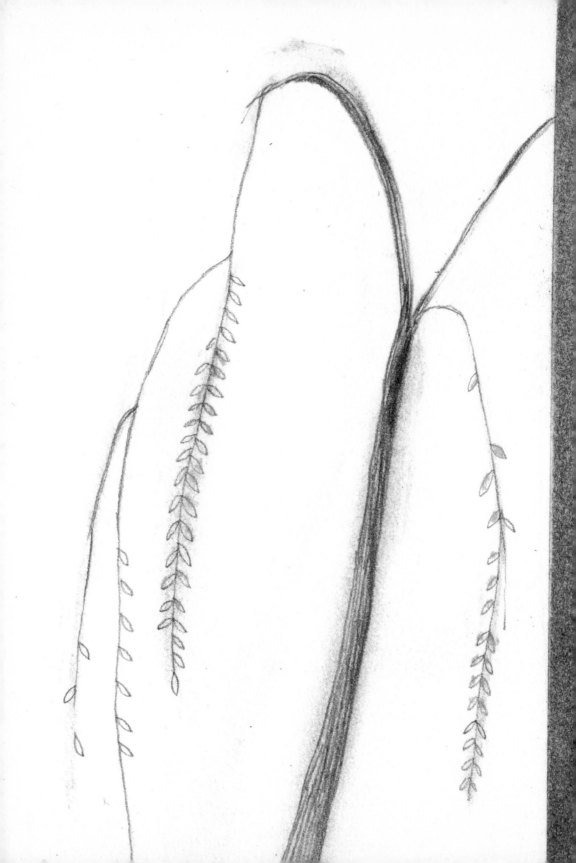

The Stories

I don't want to brag, but Death now stretches next to me on my bed over my sheets. We stay like this, without moving, like real friends. I tell Death my dreams and talk about what I'll do when I grow up.

This is what Death likes the most, me telling stories. I read to her from books my parents have given me, or I invent stories of my own.

Death likes stories about the sun. Every time I tell one her face glows, because Death is really bored in her dead life. She cannot do anything different. Death is always and will be always Death. This is her destiny.

Sometimes, at night, when she comes to stretch on my bed, I caress her face with my little hand. I wipe the cold tears running down her cheeks. I hold her tight in my arms repeating the words that I have heard thousands of times: "Don't worry… Everything will pass… One day, things will be better…"

Then Death is not so tense anymore.

She falls asleep with a smile.

Every time I hold Death in my arms I
tell myself that I could kill her. I could
knock her off with a table light, a bottle
or the basin. If Death dies, I'll save the
life of dozens of children, hundreds of
sick people, thousands of old people. But
I cannot do such a thing. I am incapable
of killing a fly.

Instead I rock Death and wait until
she wakes up.

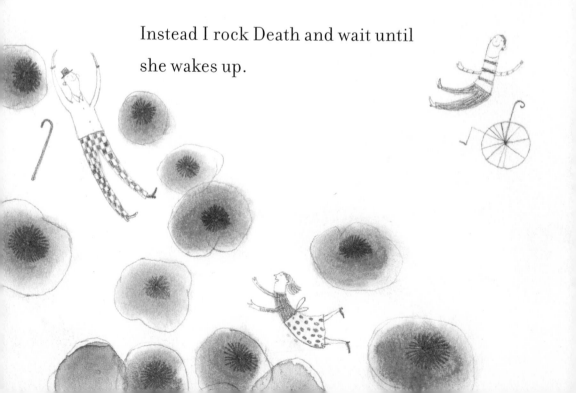

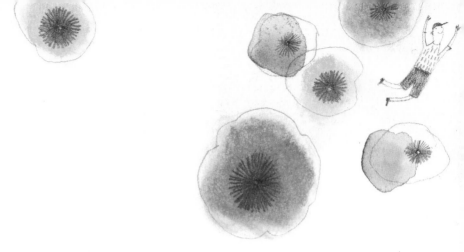

My Best Friend

Now Death and me, we are best friends. She comes to lay down under my sheets. We talk a bit before falling asleep. I learn great truths: to exist Day needs Night and Night needs Day. Heat needs Cold and Cold needs Heat. Noise needs Silence and Silence needs Noise. Death needs Life and Life needs Death. They are two inseparable friends.

A long, long time ago they made a deal:

Death takes away the dying to make room for Life. Death is definitely the best friend of Life.

I understand all this but I ask Death to wait before taking me away. It's not for me. I think about my parents. They are not ready. They will not survive my departure. So, day after day, week after week, I slowly prepare my parents. I explain to them how the big wheel of Life turns. I explain to them how the day needs the night, the heat needs the cold and how Life needs Death. But my father and my mother don't want to understand. They are afraid of absence and emptiness and all the tears that come with them.

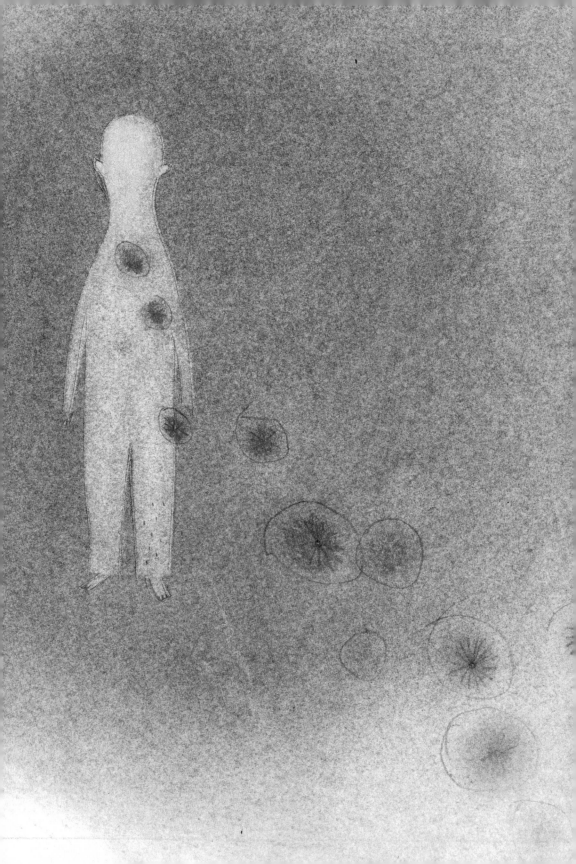

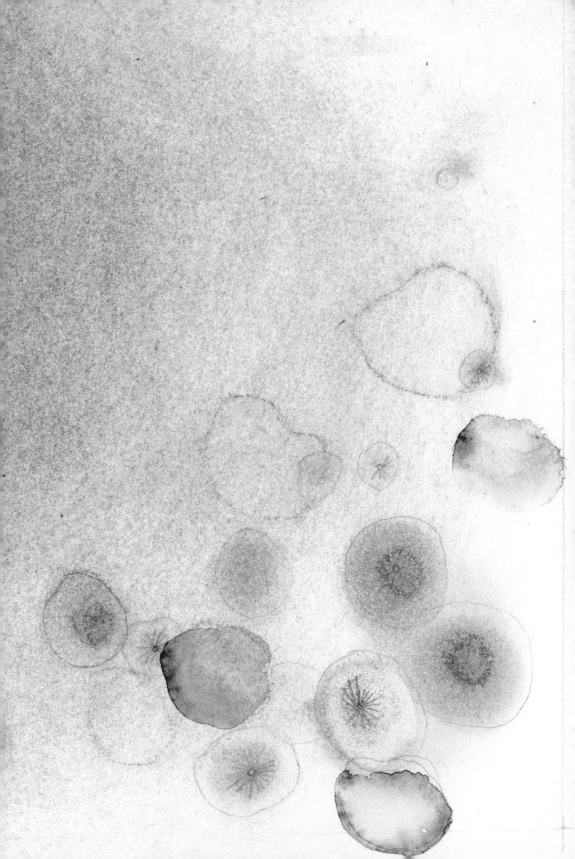

Time Passes

Death now comes to sleep with me almost every night. When she is late or doesn't come at all, I wonder what she does. I worry; I get bored. One evening, trembling from cold, Death glides under my sheets. I use the moment to ask, "When I'm in the land of dreams, where will you go to rest? Who will warm up your feet? Who will talk to you? Will you have another friend?"

I don't want to brag, but after these questions Death doesn't close her eyes all night. She thinks a lot.

The News

I changed rooms again. Sitting on my
bed, I'm very happy and very sad at the
same time. I learned good news for me,
but bad news for Death. I'm waiting for
her visit…

This evening Death is late. I hope that
nothing serious has happened to her.

Finally Death arrives at the stroke of
midnight. When I offer her a glass of

water, a slice of tart and a sweet, Death refuses. She looks nervous. She tells me we have to say our goodbyes as she's going on a long voyage.

I respond by holding her hand. "I also have bad news for you. Because of a new medicine I'll be soon cured. In a few weeks, my hair will grow again. I'll become a child like the others!"

I think that Death already knew this. She starts to cry with tears of joy. We embrace each other and we stay still all night.

When I wake up in the morning Death is gone. A little present is on my pillow.

With my heart beating, I untie the silk cord. I unwrap the paper. I open the box. It is empty. There is nothing inside. Only a few words are scribbled under the lid:

Good day! This box is magic, like Life. You can put in it your days and nights, your joys and sorrows, your laughs and your silences...

Your friend, who loves you.
X X X

Epilogue

One evening after my last treatment my parents come to collect me. With smiles on their faces they open a big suitcase to put in my toys, clothes and medicine. I hide the magic box inside and, one after the other, kiss the doctors, the nurses, the attendants and even the janitor. I leave the hospital with my cheeks wet from the tears of everyone who cared for me.

With a beating heart, I enter my house and run to my room. I have grown up so much in two years, you could say that all my toys have shrunk. I lie on my bed, with my teddy bears. Together we listen to my father and my mother telling us in turns my favorite story, about a little wolf who survives all the dangers.

My parents embrace me again and again. I close my eyes and fall asleep. I dream about my friend Death. I'm a bit bored, but I know that one day we'll find each other again.

Early the next morning, I wake up with a jump. I leave my bed, pass by my parents' room, open the door that leads to the garden and… I run in the fresh grass in my bare feet.

The birds are singing.

The sun is coming up on the horizon.

I throw myself in the arms of Life.
I don't want to brag, but I want to
live Life treasuring every moment!